THIS WALKER BOOK
BELONGS TO:

. . . .

. . . .

. . . .

For Will and Justin, again

First published 2012 by Walker Books Ltd
87 Vauxhall Walk, London SE11 5HJ

This edition published 2014

2 4 6 8 10 9 7 5 3 1

© 2012 Jon Klassen

The right of Jon Klassen to be identified as author/illustrator of this work has
been asserted by him in accordance with the Copyright, Designs and Patents Act 1988

This book has been typeset in New Century Schoolbook

Printed in China

British Library Cataloguing in Publication Data:
a catalogue record for this book is available from the British Library

ISBN 978-1-4063-5343-3

www.walker.co.uk

THIS IS NOT MY HAT

JON KLASSEN

WALKER BOOKS

AND SUBSIDIARIES

LONDON • BOSTON • SYDNEY • AUCKLAND

This hat is not mine.
I just stole it.

I stole it from a big fish.

He was asleep when I did it.

And he probably won't wake up for a long time.

And even if he does wake up,

he probably won't notice that it's gone.

And even if he does notice that it's gone,

he probably won't know it was me who took it.

And even if he does guess it was me,

he won't know where I am going.

But I will tell you where I am going.
I am going where the plants grow
big and tall and close together.

It is very hard to see in there.
Nobody will ever find me.

There is someone who has seen me.
But he said he wouldn't tell anyone
which way I went.

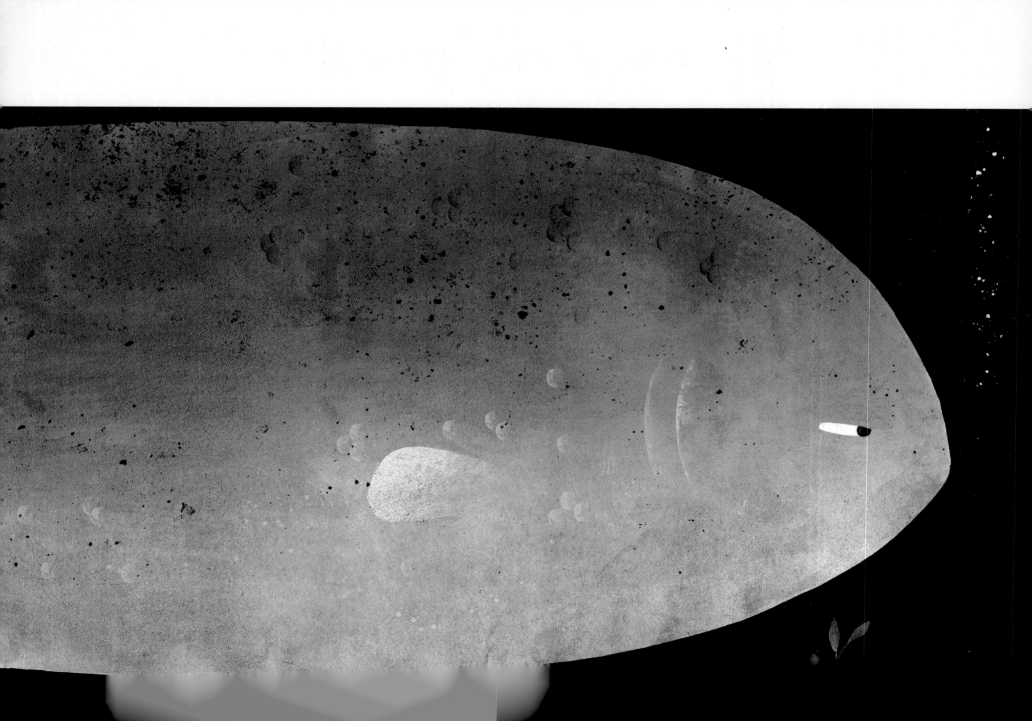

So I am not worried about that.

I know it's wrong to steal a hat.
I know it does not belong to me.
But I am going to keep it.
It was too small for him anyway.
It fits me just right.

And look! I made it!

Where the plants are big and tall and close together!

I knew I was going to make it.

Nobody will ever find me.

JON KLASSEN worked as an illustrator on the animated feature film *Coraline*. In 2010 he won the Canadian Governor General's Award for children's literature (illustration). The first book he both wrote and illustrated, *I Want My Hat Back*, was a multiple-award-winner, short-listed for the Kate Greenaway Medal and an international bestseller – as is this, its successor, winner of the prestigious Caldecott Medal. Originally from Niagara Falls, Canada, Jon now lives in the USA, in Los Angeles.

Praise for
This Is Not My Hat:

ISBN 978-1-4063-3853-9

www.walker.co.uk

www.burstofbeaden.com